Brock Cole

The Money We'll Save

Margaret Ferguson Books
FARRAR STRAUS GIROUX
New York

For Molly, Norah,

Annabelle, and William

Distributed in Canada by D&M Publishers, Inc.
Color separations by KHL Chroma Graphics
Printed in June 2011 in China by Macmillan Production (Asia) Ltd.,
Kwun Tong, Kowloon, Hong Kong (supplier code WKT)
First edition, 2011
1 3 5 7 9 10 8 6 4 2

mackids.com

Library of Congress Cataloging-in-Publication Data

Cole, Brock.

The money we'll save / Brock Cole. — 1st ed.

p. cm.

Summary: When Pa brings home a young turkey in hopes of saving money on their Christmas dinner, his family faces all sorts of trouble—and expense—in their tiny flat in a nineteenth-century New York City apartment building.

ISBN: 978-0-374-35011-6

[1. Family life—New York (State)—New York—Fiction. 2. Apartment houses—Fiction. 3. Turkeys—Fiction. 4. Christmas—Fiction. 5. New York (N.Y.)—History—19th century—Fiction.] I. Title. II. Title: The money we'll save.

PZ7.C67342Mon 2011
[E]—dc22

2010037760

Ma needed two eggs and a half pound of flour so she could make pancakes for supper, but who could she send to the market?

All the children were busy. Bailey was in the bedroom putting baby Arthur down for a nap.

Bridget was in the parlor pulling basting threads from one of the coats Ma was making for the wholesale trade.

Pearl was on the fire escape hanging out the laundry.

So Ma decided to send Pa.

"Now just buy two eggs and a half pound of flour," she told him. "Remember, Christmas is not far off, and we must save every penny."

"I'll remember," said Pa, and he set off with a shopping basket and purse.

Oh, the market was filled with temptations: great loaves of bread, cakes and pies, fat hams and sausages, and mounds of apples and potatoes. Still Pa resisted.

At the grocer's he bought a half pound of flour and not an ounce more.

From the chicken man he bought two eggs and wouldn't buy another even though it was cracked and offered cheap.

"Christmas is not far off, and we must save every penny if we're to have a proper Christmas dinner," he explained to the chicken man.

"Oh," said the chicken man, "if it's a fine dinner and saving pennies you want, I can tell you how to do that."

"How?" asked Pa.

And the chicken man told him.

“What’s that?” said Ma when Pa got back to the flat.

“That? That’s a turkey poult,” said Pa. “I bought it from the chicken man. It will fatten up into a fine bird, and we can have it for Christmas dinner. Think of the money we’ll save!”

"But where will we keep it and what will we feed it? Oh, you foolish man, wasting our money like that, and just before Christmas."

"Now calm down, dear. The chicken man said it could live in a box by the stove, and we can feed it table scraps. It will grow big and fat and cost nothing at all. Just wait. You'll see."

So the bird lived in a wooden box by the stove, and the children fed him table scraps.

They named him Alfred.

Alfred grew and grew.

Soon he was too big for his box,

and he wasn't content
with table scraps.

"Ma!" cried Bailey. "Alfred stole baby Arthur's biscuit!"

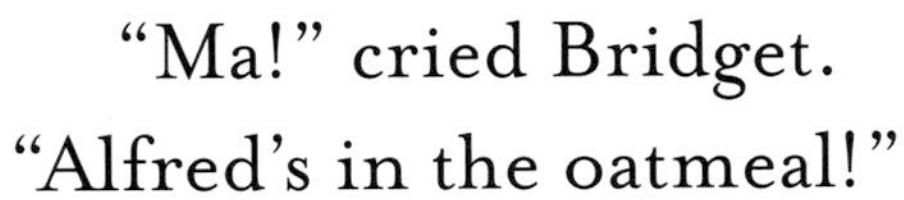

"Ma!" cried Bridget. "Alfred's in the oatmeal!"

"Ma!" cried Pearl. "Alfred's messed on the clean ironing, and it's all got to be washed again!"

Ma sat down with her face in her apron and began to cry. “I knew I should never have let that bird in the door!” she sobbed. “He’s a mess and a glutton. He’s eating us out of house and home!”

“Now, Ma,” said Pa. “It’s not long until Christmas. I’ll tell you what I’ll do. I’ll make him a pen on the fire escape and then he’ll be out of the way, and remember the money we’re saving!”

So Pa built a pen on the fire escape, and for a time everything was peaceful in the flat.

But then Mrs. Schumacher came up from downstairs and pounded on the door.

"Now where am I to get a breath of fresh air with that great bird doing his business all over the fire escape and gobbling night and day so no one can sleep?" she demanded.

Mrs. Schumacher was a fierce scold, so Pa promised to move Alfred and his pen off the fire escape.

“Now what are we to do?” cried Ma. “Shall we keep it in the bedroom? Is that your idea?”

“No, no, dear,” said Pa. “Here’s what we’re going to do. We’ll hang the pen on the clothesline! I don’t know why I didn’t think of that before. That way he won’t be a bother to anyone, and remember the money we’re saving.”

That's exactly what Pa did. He bought some pulleys and hung Alfred's pen on the clothesline and ran it out over the privies during the day and pulled it back into the kitchen at night. All was calm for a week.

But the neighbors began to complain that it wasn't safe to go out in the yard without an umbrella.

And then the clothesline broke, and the pen fell down, and Alfred broke out and chased the cats and pecked the dogs and wouldn't let Mrs. Schumacher use the privies.

There were so many complaints and so much extra washing that when Pa and the children caught Alfred there was nothing to do but bring him back into the flat.

"It's just for a few days, now," Pa explained to Ma. "And that idea you had about the bedroom was a good one. We'll move all the beds into the kitchen and parlor and give the bedroom to the bird. That way he won't be a bother, and remember the money we're saving."

And so for another week the family lived in the kitchen and the parlor, and Alfred lived in the bedroom.

Except when he got out.

And Mrs. Schumacher came upstairs three times a day: once to complain about the noise, once to complain about the smell, and once to complain about her back and her feet and how hard it was for a woman her age to climb up and down all those stairs three times a day.

Finally it was the day before Christmas.

"Well, dears," said Pa after breakfast. "Today I'll take the bird to the butcher and tomorrow we'll have him for dinner. All our troubles will be past, and think of the money we've saved."

"What bird?" asked the children.

"That bird," said Pa. "Alfred."

"What?" cried Bailey. "We can't eat Alfred!"

"It would be like eating a friend," said Bridget.

"Well," said Pearl, "not a friend, exactly. It would be like eating Mrs. Schumacher."

"Yes!" shouted Bailey and Bridget. "Do you want us to eat Mrs. Schumacher for Christmas dinner?"

"But what are we to do?" cried Pa. "Do you want him to live here? With us? Forever?"

No one wanted that. So . . .

They decided to give Alfred to Mrs. Schumacher as a Christmas present.

She was very pleased. She was a widow and, when all was said and done, she was glad of the company. What with his messes and eating everything in sight, Alfred reminded her not a little of the late Mr. Schumacher.

That Christmas Eve Ma and Pa and all the children scrubbed and scrubbed and scrubbed before they put up a very little tree from the market with no more decoration than two candles and a tin star on top.

All the pennies in the purse had been spent on pens and pulleys and laundry soap, so the next day there was nothing to eat but oatmeal with a bit of brown sugar. But the flat was clean and neat, and each child had a present, if only a little one, and the oatmeal was delicious.

"But it isn't much of a holiday feast, is it?" said Pa sadly.

"Ah, but think of the money we saved," said Ma, and she gave him a kiss because it was Christmas.